Hospital Journal

HOSPITAL JOURNAL

BY ANN BANKS
Illustrated by Cathy Bobak

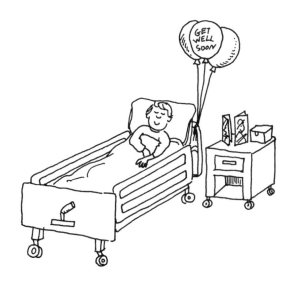

Puffin Books

I would like to thank the people who gave me advice and encouragement in preparing *Hospital Journal:* Pat Azarnoff, Pediatric Projects, Inc.; Meg Dean, St. Vincent's Hospital, New York City; Richard Thompson, Child Life Council; Jerriann Wilson, Association of Children in Hospitals; and Susan Wojtasik, Bellevue Hospital, New York City. Joanne Bernstein made thoughtful suggestions and helped with the jokes.

PUFFIN BOOKS
Published by the Penguin Group
Viking Penguin, a division of Penguin Books USA Inc.,
40 West 23rd Street, New York, New York 10010, U.S.A.
Penguin Books Ltd, 27 Wrights Lane, London W8 5TZ, England
Penguin Books Australia Ltd, Ringwood, Victoria, Australia
Penguin Books Canada Ltd, 2801 John Street, Markham, Ontario, Canada L3R 1B4
Penguin Books (N.Z.) Ltd, 182–190 Wairau Road, Auckland 10, New Zealand

Penguin Books Ltd, Registered Offices: Harmondsworth, Middlesex, England
First published in Puffin Books 1989

Published simultaneously in Canada

1 3 5 7 9 10 8 6 4 2
Text copyright © Ann Banks, 1989
Illustrations copyright © Cathy Bobak, 1989
All rights reserved

Printed in U.S.A.
by
Set in Times Roman.

Pediatric wards are becoming much more responsive to the emotional needs of children because of the efforts of concerned professionals—Child Life specialists, pediatric nurses, social workers, and pediatricians. This book is dedicated to them.

Contents

Paste a picture of yourself here

This is Me
And this is My Book.

My name: _____

My age: _____

My birthday: _____

My grade: _____

My weight: _____

My height: _____

My blood type: _____

The school I go to is: _____

The name of my town is: _____

The state we live in is: _____

Today's date: _____

About This Book

Sooner or later, nearly everyone has to go to the hospital. It might be because they're sick or in pain. It might be because they need an operation or some other kind of medical treatment. Or it could be that the doctors need to do tests to learn more about what's wrong. No matter what the reason, when you learn you have to go to the hospital, you'll probably feel worried.

Until you get used to it, the hospital can seem like a frightening place, full of strange sounds, smells, and scary-looking machines. There will be new rules to learn. You'll have to sleep away from home. The food will be different from what you usually eat. You'll be wondering about the things that may hurt.

The more you talk about what's on your mind, and the more you know in advance about what will happen, the easier it will be. (Of course, it's impossible to plan ahead if you end up in the hospital because of an accident or emergency. But with some help from your parents, most of the activities in *Hospital Journal* can be started once you're already there.)

If you ask around, you'll probably find out that your parents, your teachers, and even some of your classmates have spent time in the hospital. The nurses and doctors took care of them and helped them to get better so they could go home again. The nurses and doctors at the hospital you go to will do the same for you. That is their job. A hospital is a place where everyone works together to help you get well.

The activities in *Hospital Journal* will keep you busy while you're in the hospital, and they'll help you remember once you're home again. When you go back to school, the other kids will want to know what happened to you and how you felt about it. If you write it all down, it will be easier to share your experiences, and maybe you can help others who have to go through the same thing. When it's completed, *Hospital Journal* will be a scrapbook of your hospital stay, and a reminder of how well you managed and how brave you were.

It can be scary to go to the hospital for the first time. But you can learn a lot of good things about yourself, too. Think of your stay in the hospital as an adventure story. There will be problems—there always are in a story. But people will help you. And there are also lots of ways you can help yourself. As you put your mind to solving the problems, you'll see that the special hero of the story is *you*.

Before I Go

All About Me

The best thing that happened to me this year was _____

_____

_____

When people give me presents, the thing I most like to get is _____

_____

because _____

The thing I least like to get is _____

_____

because _____

MY FAVORITE THINGS:

Television show _____

Singer _____

Movie star _____

Book _____

Hobby _____

Sport _____

School subject _____

Animal _____

Car _____

Ribbit

My Family

My mother's name is_____

What she and I like to do together is_____

_____

She's been in the hospital before. Yes_____No_____

What she says about it is_____

_____

_____

Her job is_____

Her phone number at work is_____

←—MOTHER

FATHER—→

My father's name is_____

What he and I like to do together is_____

_____

He's been in the hospital before. Yes_____No_____

What he says about it is_____

_____

_____

His job is_____

His phone number at work is_____

My Family

I have_____brothers and_____sisters.

Their names and ages are_____

_____

What my brother(s) and I like to do together is_____

_____

_____

What my sister(s) and I like to do together is_____

_____

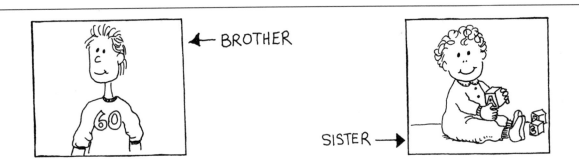

Paste or draw a picture of your family here.

My Friends

Maybe you'll want to call or write to your best friends while you're in the hospital. Fill in each friend's name, address, and phone number.

Name: _____

Address: _____

_____

Telephone Number: _____

Name: _____

Address: _____

_____

Telephone Number: _____

Name: _____

Address: _____

_____

Telephone Number: _____

Name: _____

Address: _____

_____

Telephone Number: _____

My Friends

Name: _____

Address: _____

_____

Telephone Number: _____

Name: _____

Address: _____

_____

Telephone Number: _____

Name: _____

Address: _____

_____

Telephone Number: _____

Finding Out About the Hospital

Before you go to the hospital, you'll have lots of questions about what the place is like and what will happen to you there. In fact, you'll probably keep thinking of new questions all the time. It's important to make sure you get answers. The best way to remember your questions is to write them down as soon as you think of them.

While you're getting ready to go to the hospital, you can talk things over with your parents. In the hospital, the nurses and doctors also can answer questions and discuss worries. They have many people to take care of, and sometimes they won't be able to spend much time with you. But let them know you'd like to talk, anyway. Maybe they can come back when they're not so busy.

The hospital I'm going to is:

Name: _____

Address: _____

_____

Telephone number: _____

It is_____miles from where I live.

I will probably be there about_____days, and I will miss_____days of school.

I am going into the hospital_____days from today.

The times my mom will be with me in the hospital are_____

_____

When she's not there, she will be_____

The times my dad will be with me in the hospital are_____

_____

When he's not there, he will be_____

My brothers and sisters will be visiting me in the hospital. Yes_____ No_____

Finding Out About the Hospital

The times of day they will visit are_____

Other people who might come to visit me are_____

_____

I will be staying in a room with_____other children.

We will have our meals: On a tray in bed_____ At a table_____

The times of our meals will be: Breakfast_____o'clock

                                     Lunch_____o'clock

                                     Dinner_____o'clock

I will wear: My own pajamas_____ Pajamas from the hospital_____

Will there be a telephone I can use? Yes_____ No_____

Will there be a TV in the room? Yes_____ No_____

Will there be a playroom nearby for children? Yes_____ No_____

My other questions about the hospital are:
   (Use an extra sheet of paper if you need more room.)

  *_____

_____

  *_____

_____

Getting Ready

What do you want to pack in your suitcase? Pretend you're already there and think of what you'd like to have with you. There may be some things that are against the hospital rules, so find out ahead of time. Be sure to pack *Hospital Journal*.

- ☐ Favorite pajamas and clothes
- ☐ Books
- ☐ Magazines

- ☐ School work
- ☐ Favorite pillow or blanket
- ☐ Pictures of family and pets

- ☐ Stuffed animal
- ☐ Deck of cards
- ☐ Paper (stationery, blank pages, notebooks)

- ☐ Clock or watch
- ☐ My own food
- ☐ Masking tape (for decorating your room with cards and posters)

- ☐ Pens and pencils; pencil sharpener
- ☐ Postcards and stamps
- ☐ Address book
- ☐ Puzzles and other games

- ☐ _____
- ☐ _____
- ☐ _____

Getting Ready

Tips:

Will there be a pay phone that you can use? If so, bring a list of phone numbers of friends and relatives and a stack of coins.

★ If there will be a TV you can watch, bring a schedule of your favorite programs.

★ If you have a tape recorder with earphones, you'll be able to listen to song or story tapes without bothering others. Maybe your mom or dad or your brothers or sisters can make a special tape for you to listen to while you're in the hospital.

★ Is there a camera you can bring? If so, you can take pictures of nurses, doctors, your hospital room, and your roommates.

★ Talk to your teacher about what work you'll be missing at school. Maybe you can catch up on some of it while you're resting in bed. There may even be a teacher in the hospital who can work with you.

There probably will be people who'll want to write or call you while you're in the hospital. Friends. Your grandparents. Kids in your class. So they'll know where to find you, get some cards and write down your name, the address and phone number of the hospital, how long you'll be there, and what the visiting hours are. You can give these to the people you'd like to hear from. Don't forget to give one to your teacher.

What Will Happen to Me in the Hospital?

People go to the hospital for many reasons. And there are many different ways of helping them get better. It's important to understand why you're going to the hospital and what is likely to happen to you when you are there.

Also, you'll be meeting other children who are in the hospital for a different reason. You may wonder if what happens to them will happen to you. Probably not. But the best way to find out for sure is to talk to your parents or your nurse or doctor.

Whatever you're wondering about, don't be afraid to ask! If you're not sure you understand what you're hearing, ask again. Keep asking as many times as you need to. Say, "What does that mean?" or "Could you explain that to me another way?"

The way I learned I had to go to the hospital is_____

_____

_____

The reason I am going to the hospital is_____

_____

_____

The plan for helping me get healthy again is_____

_____

_____

_____

My ideas for how I can help myself get better are_____

_____

_____

_____

12

What Will Happen to Me in the Hospital?

My other questions about what will happen are:
  (Use an extra sheet of paper if you need more room.)
  *_____

_____

  *_____

_____

  *_____

_____

  *_____

_____

  *_____

_____

Will It Hurt?

Many of the things that will happen to you in the hospital won't hurt. But there are some that will, and it's better to find out about them ahead of time. That way, you won't be taken by surprise. Usually, the pain won't last long, and it's helping to make you better.

When you're ready, talk to your mom and dad or to your doctor about things that you need to be prepared for. Write them down here.

What Can I Do About It?

When you're scared because something is going to hurt, there are things you can do. You can get the feelings out by talking to someone. That almost always helps. Or, you can cry. Even if you hardly ever cry at home, you might feel like it in the hospital. It doesn't mean you're a crybaby, and there's no reason to feel ashamed about it.

Something else you can do is to concentrate your mind on making the pain go away. Think about where the pain is in your body. Then take a deep breath and breathe it into the part of your body that hurts. Make your breath surround the pain like a cloud. Then, when you breathe out again, imagine that you are breathing the pain right out of your body. This is a trick you can practice ahead of time with the help of your mom or dad. The more you practice it, the better it will work for you.

Another idea that works for some kids is to think about something nice. Here's how. First, make a picture in your mind of your favorite place in the whole world. Imagine how it looks and sounds and smells. Maybe it's the beach. Maybe it's an amusement park. Maybe it's your aunt and uncle's farm. Maybe it's dancing on a stage. Maybe it's even your favorite class at school. Then, pretend that you are there having fun. Pretend your favorite people are there with you. Pretend everything is just exactly the way you always wanted it to be. Or, you can remember something that was really wonderful, like your birthday party. Then, every time you're feeling bad in the hospital, you can imagine this picture in your mind.

Once you have decided on your perfect picture, write it down on this page. Then you'll have it ready when it's time to go to the hospital. You might want to ask your mom or dad to help you.

In the Hospital

Ouch!!!!!

One of the things that most people really hate—grown-ups included—is being stuck with needles. And, unfortunately, that is usually part of being in the hospital, no matter what you are there for. Sometimes the needles are used to give you medicine to make you better or make the pain go away. Sometimes they're used to take out a small amount of blood. The doctors need to test the blood so they can learn more about what's going on inside your body. (Just remember that no matter how many times they take blood, your body keeps on making more of it. So you'll always have enough.)

Whatever the reason, it hurts, and you have a right to complain about it. It can help to keep track. Every time someone in the hospital comes around with a needle, make a mark on this page. Maybe you'll decide that when you have a certain number of marks, you deserve a treat.

This is the number of times I have been stuck with a needle:

This Is Embarrassing!

There is no privacy in the hospital—or not much, anyway. This bothers just about everybody, including grown-ups who have to stay in the hospital. So when you're feeling embarrassed, and wishing some things could be more private, just remember: you're not the only one!

First, there are baths. Even though you've been taking baths by yourself for years at home, you'll probably have a helper in the hospital. The bathtubs are usually up high, so you need a boost to get in. And if you're not feeling well anyway, you may be glad you don't have to manage by yourself.

If you're feeling too sick or too tired to get up yet, a nurse will help you wash in bed. Each hospital bed has a curtain you can close to separate it from the others. The nurse will pull the curtain around your bed, so no one can see. But if she forgets, or doesn't pull it far enough, remind her. Say, "Could you please close the curtain more."

Sometimes kids who aren't allowed to get out of bed yet have to use a bedpan. This is like a potty—the nurse brings it to you and closes the curtains and you sit on it in bed. This may sound weird and embarrassing, but you get used to it. And if you can get out of bed to go to the bathroom, you won't ever need to use it.

Then there are the urine samples that just about every patient in a hospital must produce. You will be given a plastic cup or bottle and told to urinate into it. Nurses are used to helping with this, so ask for help if you want it. Or, you can do it by yourself. There's a good reason for it: by studying your urine, doctors can tell a lot about what's happening inside your body. But if you think it's gross, you have lots of company.

If it would make you feel better, you can keep track of the most embarrassing things that happen to you in the hospital. And don't forget—other kids feel the same way!

This Is Embarrassing!

It was very embarrassing when_____

_____

It was very, very embarrassing when_____

_____

It was very, very, very embarrassing when_____

_____

It was very, very, very, very, embarrassing when_____

The Best Medicine

There's an old saying that "Laughter is the best medicine." A good laugh can make you feel better than almost anything else. And sharing jokes is a good way to meet people. Here are a couple of hospital jokes. Try them out on your nurses, doctors, and roommates. And if they tell *you* any good jokes, write them down here.

What do you call a sick alligator?
An illigator.

Doctor: I want to take your appendix out this evening.
Patient: OK, but make sure it's back by midnight.

Knock, knock.
Who's there?
Isabel.
Isabel who?
Isabel the way to call the nurse?

What's the difference between a hill and a pill?
One is hard to get up and the other is hard to get down.

Knock, knock.
Who's there?
Lettuce
Lettuce who?
Lettuce see your tongue.

The Best Medicine

Why do you go to the hospital?
Because the hospital can't come to you.

How did the sick kids get to the hospital so fast?
Flu.

When is it polite to stick your tongue out at someone?
When the doctor makes you say "Ahhh."

When is the doctor most annoyed?
When he's out of patients.

Knock, knock.
Who's there?
Arthur.
Arthur who?
Arthur Mometer is broken.

Jokes I Have Heard

21

My Hospital Stay

On the calendar below, fill in the month and days that you'll be staying in the hospital. Each day that you're there, draw an X through that day on the calendar. Sometimes things change, depending on how fast you're getting better. So you might have to stay a little longer than you expected, or you might even get out sooner. Your doctor will let you go home as soon as you are well enough.

This month is _____

SUNDAY	MONDAY	TUESDAY	WEDNESDAY	THURSDAY	FRIDAY	SATURDAY

What Is That?

To measure how your body is doing, the doctors and nurses will take your temperature, your pulse, your blood pressure, and listen to your heartbeat. In helping you get well, they'll use many different kinds of equipment. You may wonder what some of the things are called and what they are for. If you're curious, ask.

Medical equipment I have seen is:

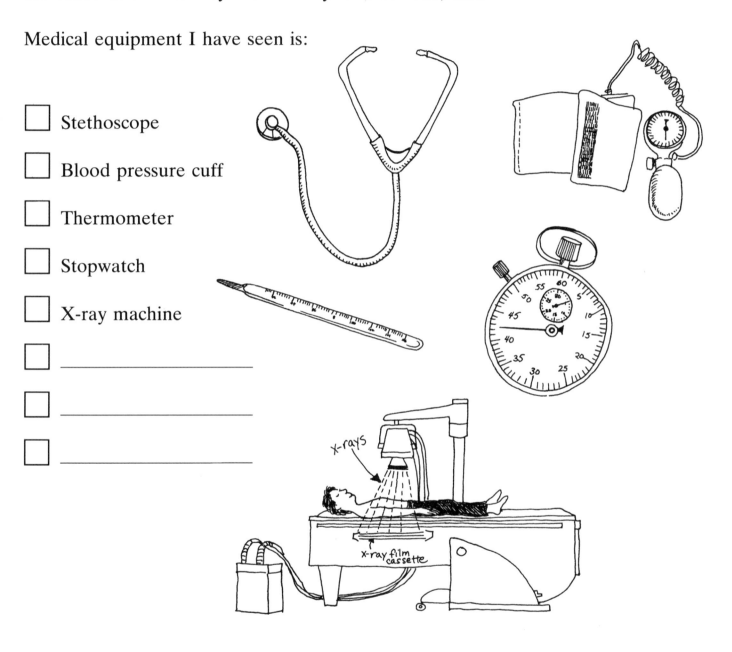

- ☐ Stethoscope
- ☐ Blood pressure cuff
- ☐ Thermometer
- ☐ Stopwatch
- ☐ X-ray machine
- ☐ _____
- ☐ _____
- ☐ _____

x-rays

x-ray film cassette

Hospital Sounds

Hospitals are full of strange noises, all day and all night. You'll hear people talking over an intercom. Doctors wear beepers that are constantly going off. There are always cleaning carts and rolling beds making a racket in the halls.

Another hospital noise you may hear is the sound of someone crying. Maybe it will be someone in another room. But even when it's one of the children in your own room, you may not see what's going on. Usually the hospital bed curtain is closed for privacy when a child is having a test or a medical treatment done. Sometimes these hurt, and so you may hear crying.

It's upsetting to hear someone cry when you don't know the reason for it. You may feel scared and wish you could help, but there isn't much you can do. If the child is someone you know, you can try to comfort him or her when whatever was hurting is over. Also, you can talk to your nurse or to your parents about what happened.

Hospital noises I have noticed: _____

_____

_____

_____

Talking Things Over

When you're worried about what might happen to you, the best people to talk to are grown-ups. Your parents. The doctors and nurses. The person whose job is to talk to and play with kids. You may hear things from other children in the hospital that will bother you. Sometimes kids tell other kids scary things that they know aren't true just to tease them. And sometimes a kid really believes something is true, but it isn't. So if another kid says anything about what will happen to you, it's important to ask a grown-up about it right away.

Also, you may wonder if something will happen to you like what you've seen on television doctor shows. It won't. Real life is very different from television. But if you're worried about it, you should talk to a grown-up.

Some of the things I wonder about:

* _____

* _____

* _____

* _____

Meeting New People

During your stay in the hospital, you'll meet many new people. The other kids in your room. Their parents. The nurses and doctors who will be taking care of you. In many hospitals, there is even someone whose job is to play with children. There are also people called lab technicians, nurse's aides, dietary aides, and housekeepers. They do things like run the machines, bring the food, and keep the place clean.

When you're back home again, you'll want to remember the people you liked. One way is to get their autographs. On this page, ask your favorite people to write their autographs and the names of their jobs.

Meeting New People

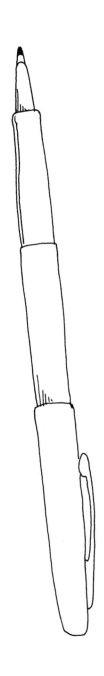

Getting to Know My Roommates

The people you'll spend the most time with in the hospital are the other kids in your room. Find out about your new roommates. Fill in the answers below.

My roommate's name: _____

Address: _____

_____

Telephone number at home: _____

Grade in school: _____

Number of brothers and sisters: _____

The reason my roommate is in the hospital is _____

_____

My roommate has been in the hospital for _____days/weeks.

What my roommate hates most about the hospital is _____

_____

One things my roomate likes about the hospital is _____

_____

My roommate's favorite things:

Television show _____   Sport _____

Singer _____   School subject _____

Movie star _____   Animal _____

Book _____   Car _____

Hobby _____

Getting to Know My Roommates

My roommate's name: _____ Age _____

Address: _____

_____

Telephone number at home: _____

Grade in school: _____ Name of school: _____

Number of brothers and sisters: _____

The reason my roommate is in the hospital is _____

_____

My roommate has been in the hospital for _____ days/weeks.

What my roommate hates most about the hospital is _____

_____

One things my roomate likes about the hospital is _____

_____

My roommate's favorite things:

Television show _____ Sport _____

Singer _____ School subject _____

Movie star _____ Animal _____

Book _____ Car _____

Hobby _____

Getting to Know My Nurses

Your parents will spend as much time with you as they can while you're in the hospital. But when they're not around, or even when they are, the nurses are always ready to take care of you and help you feel as good as possible. There are nurses who stay awake all night just in case you need them. All you have to do is press a special button by your bed and a nurse will come along and see what she or he can do to help you. So if you're thirsty, or you need help getting to the bathroom, or you're just worried about something in the night, you can just press the button to call a nurse.

You'll want to find out about your nurses. Fill in the answers below.

My nurse's name is _____

She/he is from _____

She/he lives in _____

She/he has been a nurse for_____years.

She/he decided to become a nurse because _____

_____

_____

My nurse's favorite things:

Television show _____   Hobby _____

Singer _____   Sport _____

Movie star _____   Animal _____

Book _____   Car _____

My nurse's name is _____

She/he is from _____

She/he lives in _____

She/he has been a nurse for_____years.

Getting to Know My Nurses

She/he decided to become a nurse because _____

_____

_____

My nurse's favorite things:

Television show _____   Hobby _____

Singer _____   Sport _____

Movie star _____   Animal _____

Book _____   Car _____

My nurse's name is _____

She/he is from _____

She/he lives in _____

She/he has been a nurse for _____ years.

She/he decided to become a nurse because _____

_____

_____

My nurse's favorite things:

Television show _____   Hobby _____

Singer _____   Sport _____

Movie star _____   Animal _____

Book _____   Car _____

Getting to Know My Doctors

You may talk to many different doctors while you're in the hospital. But there probably will be one or two who are in charge of taking care of you. Your parents chose them because they're good at helping kids like you get healthy again. Doctors often don't have as much time to talk to you as they'd like. But ask a few questions and see what you can find out.

Fill in the answers below.

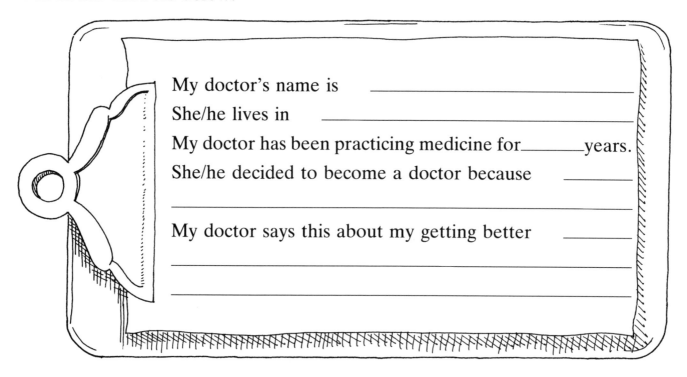

My doctor's name is _____

She/he lives in _____

My doctor has been practicing medicine for_____years.

She/he decided to become a doctor because _____

_____

My doctor says this about my getting better _____

_____

_____

My doctor's name is _____

She/he lives in _____

My doctor has been practicing medicine for_____years.

She/he decided to become a doctor because _____

_____

My doctor says this about my getting better _____

_____

_____

Getting to Know My Doctors

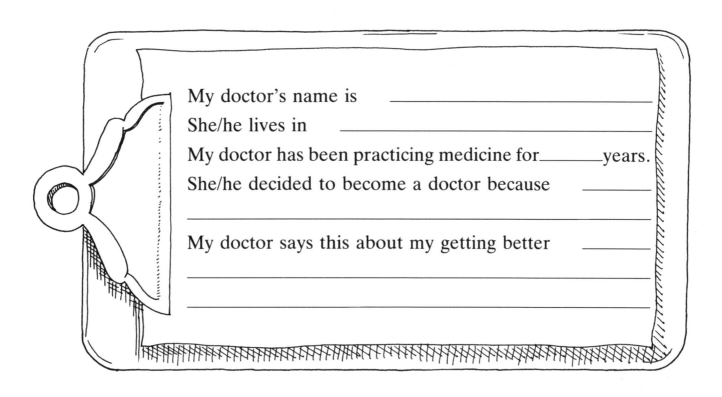

My doctor's name is _____

She/he lives in _____

My doctor has been practicing medicine for_____years.

She/he decided to become a doctor because _____

_____

My doctor says this about my getting better _____

_____

_____

My doctor's name is _____

She/he lives in _____

My doctor has been practicing medicine for_____years.

She/he decided to become a doctor because _____

_____

My doctor says this about my getting better _____

_____

_____

A Day in the Hospital

A day in the hospital has a routine, just like a day at school. Certain things happen at the same time every day.

You can add your own special routine to the regular hospital schedule. You can decide on certain times for activities like reading, playing, making phone calls, or writing in *Hospital Journal*.

On this page, fill in the schedule of a regular day.

Morning: _____

_____

_____

Afternoon: _____

_____

_____

Night: _____

_____

_____

What's to Eat Around Here?

The hospital has a big kitchen where all the food is cooked. Usually your meals are brought to you in bed on a tray. The food may be different from what you're used to, but often you have a choice of what to eat. Every day you'll be given a menu with several different selections, and you can circle what you want. Pick your favorite menu and, so you won't forget the kinds of foods you ate while you were in the hospital, paste a hospital menu on this page.

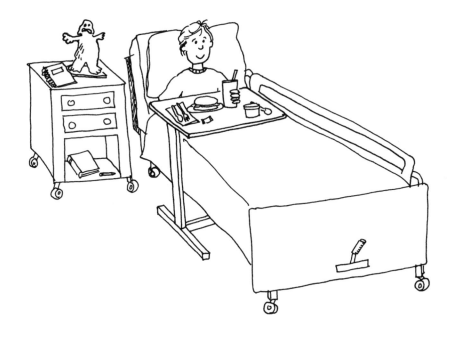

Friends and Family

The people who have come to visit me in the hospital are:

Friends and Family

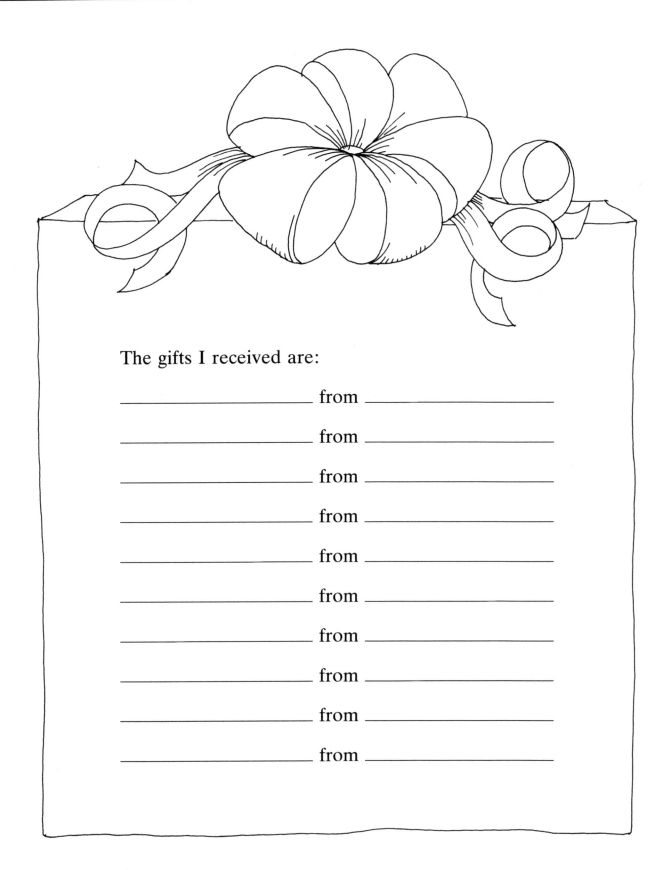

The gifts I received are:

_____ from _____

_____ from _____

_____ from _____

_____ from _____

_____ from _____

_____ from _____

_____ from _____

_____ from _____

_____ from _____

_____ from _____

Friends and Family

The People who have called me are:

Friends and Family

Use the next few pages to paste in some of the cards and pictures you received.

Hospital Likes and Dislikes

Start with the dislikes. Shots, for example. What are the things that you just absolutely hate about being in the hospital?

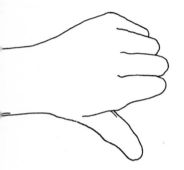

* _____

_____

* _____

_____

* _____

_____

* _____

_____

* _____

_____

Hospital Likes and Dislikes

There probably are some things you like about being in the hospital, too—all the extra attention, for example. What are they?

* _____

_____

* _____

_____

* _____

_____

* _____

_____

I'm Going Home!

Getting out of the hospital is something to look forward to. But you may not be feeling perfect again as soon as you're at home. Sometimes, kids have to rest for a while before they can go back to school or out to play.

Sooner or later, though, things will go back to the way they were. Imagine a wonderful day once you're at home. Who will you play with? What will you eat? On this page, describe what you're especially looking forward to.

When I'm Home

What Was It Like?

Other kids will want to know about what happened to you. Your brothers and sisters, your friends, and your classmates will probably all have questions. Tell them to go ahead and ask you anything they want.

Someone asked_____

_____

*I told them*_____

_____

_____

Someone asked_____

_____

*I told them*_____

_____

_____

Someone asked_____

_____

*I told them*_____

_____

_____

My Advice Is . . .

Pretend you met someone who had to go to the hospital for the same reason you did. What would you tell him or her about what to expect? What's the most important thing to know ahead of time? What was the scariest thing? What did you like best? What was it like sharing a room with other kids? How long does it take to feel better? How do you look while you're in the hospital? What should you take with you?

A Parents' Guide

A Parents' Guide

Each year about 4 million children face an overnight stay in the hospital. Children who are sick or in pain must leave behind the cozy familiarity of home and family and confront the stuff of nightmares: ominous-looking machines, strange faces, odd smells, and creepy, unexplained noises. It's invariably scary, but given the opportunity to ask questions and express their fears and fantasies, children can emerge from a hospitalization with new confidence. The renowned pediatrician and child development expert T. Berry Brazelton has written that, "If a child learns that she can cope with pain, with being in a strange, frightening place away from home, can learn how to manage for herself at times, can see that people like doctors and nurses want to help even though they hurt her—all of these can add up to a positive experience in learning how to master the world."

Using *Hospital Journal,* parents can help their school-age children make a healthy adjustment to a stressful situation. *Hospital Journal* invites children to express and order their feelings as they chronicle their hospital stay. Although many children's books have been written on the subject, there is no book that allows the child to shape his own version of the experience. *Hospital Journal* provides an opportunity for the child to learn about and describe the specific things he himself will encounter. Since the child participates in creating *Hospital Journal,* it becomes an important personal possession—one that can serve as a comfort in a strange environment. And, important to child and parent alike, it gives him something to *do* during a difficult but often boring time.

Hospital Journal will engage the child with activities before, during, and after her hospital stay—from the moment she learns she must go to the hospital, until she is convalescing at home, recalling the experience and discussing it with family and friends. In the first few pages, she will describe the familiar signposts of life at home: family, friends, likes, and dislikes. Once the child feels comfortable writing in *Hospital Journal,* she will then turn to learning about the particulars of the impending hospitalization.

Some of the activities the child will complete on his own; others are designed to be done with the help of adults. As he fills in the spaces in the book, the child will gain a sense of mastery, and be better able to discuss his feelings with you. If you take time to read the text of *Hospital Journal* now, before your child fills it in, you'll learn about the issues *you* will face during the weeks ahead.

You will find that pediatric wards have improved dramatically since hospitalizations you may have experienced as a child. In the past 15 or 20 years, hospitals have come to recognize that the emotional needs of sick children shouldn't take a backseat to their medical requirements. The pediatric staff of many hospitals now include a new type of professional with a background in child development. Sometimes called a Child Life specialist or a parent consultant, this person is trained to attend to the questions and fears of young patients, to play with them, familiarize them with hospital equipment, and prepare them for medical procedures. Programs for children vary from hospital to hospital, but there is generally a playroom stocked with toys, games, hospital equipment for playing with, and books. In some hospitals, the program includes a pre-admission orientation program and tour.

If there is a Child Life specialist in your hospital, this person usually can be counted on to understand the emotional turmoil experienced by sick children—and their parents. There is probably no better place to turn for information and advice. The suggestions that follow have been distilled from research on children in hospitals, and also from the strategies of parents and children themselves.

*Consider where you'll stay while your child is hospitalized. Most hospitals now allow parents to stay overnight with young children. Yet once children reach school age, they may prefer not having a parent stay through the night. This is because older children are usually highly social and are capable of developing relationships with other patients and the hospital staff.

If, after talking it over with all concerned, you decide not to sleep over in the hospital, there are several things to consider. Your child should know exactly where you are and how to reach you when you're not in the room. It's also important to emphasize that someone on the hospital staff is in charge of looking after her at all times, night and day. And that at night, a nurse will look into her room occasionally, just to make sure everything is all right.

*Prepare your child in advance for the hospital stay. Parents often wonder how soon to tell a child about an impending hospitalization. Most experts believe that school-age children—those old enough to fill in *Hospital Journal*—benefit from knowing several weeks in advance.

And the preparation should be thorough as well as timely. Studies over the past several decades have shown that children find vague, undefined threats more upsetting than dangers that are known and understood. Children need a careful, reassuring explanation of their illness as well as of what will happen during their hospitalization. Without such an explanation, they will devise their own strikingly inaccurate fantasies.

Don't hesitate to use scientific terminology in describing your child's diagnosis and treatment. School-age children often delight in learning the technical terms for things. And knowing more about what doctors do and how their bodies work gives them an added sense of control over what is happening to them.

*First, let your child explain it to *you*. It's important to ask a child what *he* thinks is going to happen to him, before offering reassurance. There are projects in *Hospital Journal* that are designed to encourage the child to speak his mind, and when he does, you may hear of worries that are far from what you expected. Children's concerns inevitably include fantasies, fears, and misunderstandings that need to be corrected. For example, when one young patient found himself hooked up to a heart monitor, he was convinced he was about to die. He'd seen it on television, he explained, and that's what always happened when somebody was connected to a heart monitor.

Another source of frightening misconceptions is other children. One boy deliberately disobeyed his doctor and ate breakfast the morning he was scheduled to have an operation, causing the surgery to be postponed. It emerged that older kids had teased him by telling him he'd surely die on the operating table. So he did the only thing in his power to prevent the procedure from taking place.

*Discuss medical procedures honestly, but with sensitivity. Certain subjects must be treated with care. In discussing anesthesia, for instance, children sometimes need reassurance that they won't say anything embarrassing or reveal any secrets while they are unconscious, and that they won't wake up until the operation is over. If part of their body will be removed—tonsils, appendix—they may wonder what will happen to it. And they may worry that they will no longer be the same person afterwards.

It's also good to keep in mind that a procedure that is relatively minor from a medical standpoint, can seem just as terrifying to your child as would something more serious. While outpatient surgery, increasingly common in pediatrics, avoids some of the upsets of an overnight hospital stay, many areas of potential stress remain. The activities in *Hospital Journal* dealing with the actual medical procedure, and the feelings it evokes, also can be done by children who will be hospital outpatients.

*Help your child prepare for pain. In addition to activities designed to allay fears, *Hospital Journal* describes several techniques that may help your child feel more in control. With your guidance, she can imagine—and write down—ahead of time a pleasant fantasy of a beautiful spot or a happy situation. Or she can call up the memory of an especially happy time. Then, whenever she is undergoing an unpleasant or painful procedure, she can occupy her mind with visualizing this picture. Also described in *Hospital Journal* is a simplified version of a breathing and relaxation exercise that helps some people deal with pain.

*Express confidence in the hospital staff. When you think about entrusting your child to a hospital, you will undoubtedly be faced with anxieties and questions of your own. You may feel frustrated and helpless—suddenly someone else has taken over part of your parental authority. Yet, whatever your private feelings, it's important to reassure your child that you and the medical staff are all on the same team. And that team's goal is to help her get better again. Children inevitably are distressed when they realize that their parents are no longer totally in charge of their care. But frequent parental expressions of confidence in the doctors and nurses will go a long way toward lessening that distress.

*Help your child stay in touch. The more communication he has with friends, relatives, and schoolmates while he's away in the hospital, the more secure he will feel. You can help by making sure people know how to reach him.

*Inform your child's teacher about the hospitalization. Your child may want to talk it over ahead of time with classmates. Also, to maintain as much continuity as possible, arrangements should be made for schoolwork to continue during a hospital stay. Perhaps the teacher will prepare special assignments, and agree to confer every few days by phone with your child.

*Make lists with your child of what to pack. Find out in advance what the rules are about bringing things to the hospital. Many hospitals now permit children to wear their own clothes or pajamas. And, depending on a child's medical condition, it's often possible to bring special food from home. If allowed, these two items can serve as a great comfort to your child.

She'll also want to pack some favorite belongings to remind her of home. A family photo album can provide a comforting reminder of cherished relatives, beloved pets, happy vacation times. It also can help your child get acquainted with her hospital roommates.

In addition to books, puzzles, and toys, make sure your child takes plenty of writing materials: pens and pencils, postcards and stamps, and address book. If there will be a pay phone available in the hospital, be sure to bring a list of phone numbers of friends and family, along with a stack of coins.

You may also wish to lend or give your child an inexpensive camera to take to the hospital. By documenting her new environment—taking pictures of nurses, doctors, hospital room—your child can gain a measure of control over it. These photographs can serve to remind your child of how well she got through a difficult experience.

A tape recorder with earphones can be a great comfort in the hospital. It will allow your child to listen to music or story tapes without bothering others. And family members, especially those who won't be able to visit, may want to make their own tapes for the child to take along. If you pack some blank tapes, your child can make her own audio documentary of the ward by interviewing nurses, doctors, roommates, and visitors.

*Keep brothers and sisters informed. If siblings know what's going on from the very beginning, they'll be less likely to feel left out, guilty, or frightened. Whenever possible, encourage them to help with preparations for the hospitalization. And make sure that they, too, are informed about the diagnosis and treatment, the length of the hospital stay, and if and when they will be allowed to visit.

*Ease your child's homecoming. Try to integrate your child into his usual routine as soon as possible, reinstating his responsibilities as he's capable of handling them. While it's important to acknowledge his bravery, resist making him the center of attention of the household. And don't be surprised if there are some changes in your child's behavior when he returns home from the hospital. It's not unusual for children to revert to younger behavior for a time; they may be inclined to cling more and to need extra attention. Your child needs to work through his feelings about having been ill and in the hospital, and this process may take weeks or even months.

The final activities in *Hospital Journal* are concerned with integrating the hospital experience by describing it and offering advice to others. Completed, *Hospital Journal* will have helped your child master feelings of helplessness and fear, and eased the adjustment to the hospital experience. In the months to come, it can serve as a satisfying reminder of triumph over adversity.